Lee Aucoin, *Creative Director*
Jamey Acosta, *Senior Editor*
Heidi Fiedler, *Editor*
Produced and designed by
Denise Ryan & Associates
Illustration © Holli Conger
Rachelle Cracchiolo, *Publisher*

Teacher Created Materials

5301 Oceanus Drive
Huntington Beach, CA 92649-1030
http://www.tcmpub.com
Paperback: ISBN: 978-1-4333-5449-6
Library Binding: ISBN: 978-1-4807-1128-0
© 2014 Teacher Created Materials

Playground Friends

Written by Amelia Edwards

Illustrated by Holli Conger

MW01000988

Who is at the playground today?

3

Britney is on the bars.

Bakri is on the bridge.

Sara is on the swing.

Rosa is on the rings.

I'm here, too!